# TOMMY DONBAVAND FUNNY SHORTS

# MY GRANNY BIT MY BUM

WRITTEN BY TOMMY DONBAVAND

ILLUSTRATED BY LEE ROBINSON

Franklin Watts
First published in Great Britain in 2016 by The Watts Publishing Group

Text copyright © Tommy Donbavand 2016
Illustration copyright © The Watts Publishing Group 2016

Credits
Executive Editor: Adrian Cole
Design Manager: Peter Scoulding
Cover Designer: Cathryn Gilbert
Illustrator: Lee Robinson

HB ISBN 978 1 4451 4617 1
PB ISBN 978 1 4451 4633 1
Library ebook ISBN 978 1 4451 4618 8

Printed in China

MIX
Paper from
responsible sources
FSC
www.fsc.org  FSC® C104740

Franklin Watts
An imprint of
Hachette Children's Group
Part of The Watts Publishing Group
Carmelite House
50 Victoria Embankment
London EC4Y 0DZ

An Hachette UK Company
www.hachette.co.uk

www.franklinwatts.co.uk

# Contents

# Chapter One:
# Bite!

It started out as an average Sunday. I slept in, watched some TV, did my homework. Then we all went round to my granny and granddad's house for the evening.

But things got weird after we'd finished our dinner. My dad and granddad were dozing off in front of a snooker match on TV. My mum and granny were in the kitchen, making another pot of tea and having a natter about whatever it is women talk about when they're alone. Knitting probably, and their husbands. And soup. I dunno.

As for me — I was sprawled across the floor in front of the electric fire, reading a story on a local news website. Two men had robbed a corner shop near my school! Apparently, they'd burst in, tied up the owner and stolen all the money from the till. And they'd got away with it, too.

The article described the men, saying one was tall and thin, and the other was short and chubby. And it said they were both very dangerous and should not be approached by members of the public.

Wow! Nothing like that ever happens around here. I've lived in this town ever since I was born, and the most exciting thing I can remember was when Uncle Henry found a boa constrictor snake in his back garden. Animal rescue turned up to catch it, plus three ambulances in case anyone ended up bitten. Or constricted. The 'snake' turned out to be a bit of garden hose with a dead mouse stuck in one end.

So, there I was, reading about a real-life local action story, when my granny's cat — Mr Grimsdale — waddled over. He usually lies in front of the fire, and I think he was a bit jealous of me taking his spot 'cos he kept nudging me in the ribs with his head.

I tried to push him away a couple of times, but he's so fat the best I could do was roll him onto his back. He seemed happy enough with that and stayed there.

That's when my granny came in with a glass of lemonade and a plate of Jammie Dodger biscuits for me.

"Here you go, William, love!"

"Gran!" I said. "Please call me Billy. All my friends do."

"Nothing wrong with a good name like William," she said.

"Except it makes me sound seventy years old," I pointed out.

My gran just winked and stepped over to put my drink down. But she didn't spot Mr Grimsdale lolling about, and she accidentally stood on his tail. It must have hurt, because the cat screeched so loud it made my brain buzz.

My granny jumped back, dumping half a dozen Jammie Dodgers and a glass of lemonade into my sleeping dad's lap. He shot up in the air, showering Granddad with what was left of his lukewarm cup of tea.

Granddad shouted "Peanuts!" (I've no idea why), and threw a cushion at the TV. It missed, but hit my granny on the back of her head. That knocked her false teeth out of her mouth and sent them flying — and they bit me hard right on my bum.

I didn't know it at the time, but things were soon going to get a lot worse...

CHOMP!

The following morning, I was walking to school with my best friend, Owen. You'd like Owen — he's funny, but a bit weird. He loves monsters, like mummies and zombies, but he thinks vampires are real and disguised as late-night road sweepers.

Told you. Weird.

Anyway, I was telling Owen about the bite on my bum just as we passed the Post Office. Mr Khan, the owner, was opening up early so the long queue of people waiting outside could get warm.

"Good morning, Owen and William!" he called out as we passed, switching on his bright shop sign. I opened my mouth to reply but, suddenly, I started to feel a bit ... strange.

I told Owen so.

"I feel a bit strange," I said.

Owen frowned. "Have you got, like, a buzzing noise in your head?" he asked.

"Yeah," I said, nodding. "Now you come to mention it, I have!"

"I bet your arms and legs feel stiff," Owen said.

"That's right!" I agreed.

"And your eyes?"

"What about them?"

"Are they really, really itchy — like you just want to claw them out of their sockets with your bare fingers, then throw them on the floor and stamp them into the ground, spreading sticky, gooey eye juice everywhere?"

I blinked. "No, not really."

"Don't know what your problem is then," said Owen. "Sorry."

Fat lot of help he was!

Then my body went all wonky.

My spine twisted and bent forwards, my ears grew larger, and a faint moustache sprouted on my top lip. My hair turned grey — with a pink tint — and my fingernails were long and painted a pale, shimmering gold.

Even my clothes changed! One minute I was wearing my usual boring school uniform. The next, I was dressed in a sensible coat, a chiffon headscarf and a pair of boots that appeared to be made from yeti skin.

Oh, and I was carrying the heaviest handbag in the universe.

The transformation complete, I threw back my head and shouted: "Young people of today have no respect for their elders!"

And then I did a really loud, incredibly stinky fart.

"What's happened to me?" I croaked.

"I don't know how to tell you this, Billy," said Owen with a gulp. "But I think you're a were-granny!"

# Chapter Two:
# Billy!

"A were-what?" I demanded — and jumped at the sound of my own voice. It was a lot more high-pitched than I remembered it.

"A were-granny!" said Owen. "You know — like a werewolf, but with old lady bits instead of fangs and fur."

"Do were-grannies even exist?"

Owen shrugged. "I've never heard of one," he said. "But then, I've never seen my best mate transform into an old age pensioner right in front of me before."

I shuffled as quickly as I could to the hair salon next door to the Post Office, and turned to examine my reflection in the window. It was weird seeing someone else — an elderly woman — staring back at me instead of the usual-looking boy. When I blinked, she blinked. When I turned to the side, she did the same.

I briefly wondered what she would do if I tried a karate move.

"Did anyone else see what happened?" I asked. "Mr Khan, or anyone in the Post Office queue?"

"I don't think so," said Owen. "They were all too keen to get inside out of the cold."

"It is a bit nippy out today," I said, pulling my coat around me. "I wonder if Mr Khan's got all four bars of his shop heater on..."

Owen giggled. "You're starting to sound like a granny as well now!"

I sighed. "Why has this happened?" I said. "And how?"

"It must have been that bite you got from your granny's false teeth," Owen said. "You've been infected with old lady DNA. Probably."

"But, I was bitten last night," I pointed out. "Why didn't I transform then? Why wait until now?"

"Werewolves don't change when they're first bitten, either," said Owen. "They only get hairy when the full moon is out..." He peered up at the sky.

"I doubt there's going to be a full moon out at..." I paused to check the clock in the Post Office window, "...quarter-to-nine in the morning."

"Quarter-to-nine!" said Owen. "We'd better get a move on if we don't want to be late for school."

"I can't go to school looking like this!" I cried. "I'm at least 50 years too old!"

Owen nodded. "I'm pretty sure you'd lose your place on the football team, too."

"So, what do we do?"

"Something must have triggered your transformation," said Owen, thinking hard. "Like the moon does with a werewolf..."

My eyes grew wide, the glittery eyeshadow sparkling. "And if we can work out what that trigger was, we might be able to find a way to reverse it!" I exclaimed.

"OK," said Owen, pacing up and down. "You went all granny about ten minutes ago, just as we passed the queue outside the Post Office." He stopped and looked at me. "Do you think one of them cast a spell on you?"

"They're old people, Owen," I said. "Not witches and wizards..."

"Alright, then... Mr Khan said good

morning, didn't he?"

"Then he switched on the Post Office
sign..."

We both froze.

"The light from the Post Office sign!"
I gasped. "It shone on me just like the
moon does on werewolves!"

"Come on, then," urged Owen, grabbing my arm. "Let's get you away from that light."

We couldn't move very quickly — well, I couldn't move very quickly — but our idea seemed to work. The further we got from the Post Office and its bright red and yellow sign, the more I began to feel like myself again.

My back straightened up, the wrinkles smoothed out of my skin, and my hair reverted to its usual mop of brown. I felt the layers of make-up melting away (which was very weird), my fingernails were once again bitten too far down, and my upper lip was quickly hair-free!

By the time we reached the school gates even my uniform was back in place.

"We did it!" I grinned.

Owen checked his watch. "Yeah, but we're ten minutes late for double history. We're going to get a detention from Mr Parker."

"Trust me," I said. "It's better than going granny!"

But we didn't have to worry about detention in the end. When we finally got to class, there was a new figure taking the register: a young man in a badly fitting suit. "Come along, boys, hurry up!" he said as we crashed in through the door.

"Where's Mr Parker?" I asked.

"He's off sick," said the new guy. "I'm Mr Wells, your supply teacher for the day. Now, take your seats while I finish the register."

Owen and I shared a high-five as we made our way to our seats at the back of the room. We'd solved my pesky pensioner problem, avoided detention for being late — and now we were going to have fun winding up the poor, unsuspecting supply teacher.

"Now," said Mr Wells, opening the register again. "Where were we ... ah yes ... Rachel Shields?"

"Here, sir."

"Yousuf Usman?"

"Sir!"

"William Tucker?"

"You can call me Billy if you like, sir!" I said with a grin. But my smile fell as I reached into my rucksack for my pencil case. My bag was filled with boiled sweets, packets of tissues and a carefully folded raincoat, covered with a flowery design.

Cautiously, I pulled my hand back above the desk. The skin was all wrinkly, and my nails were long and painted gold.

"Owen!" I hissed, but he was already staring at me in horror.

"Whatever your trigger is, it's not the Post Office sign!" he gulped. "You're transforming again!"

33

# Chapter Three:
# Bluff!

Thankfully, Owen and I sat right at the back of the class in history — so everyone was facing away from us when I transformed. Mr Wells also had his back to us, writing today's topic — the Second World War — on the board.

So, no one saw me shrink back into my old lady form. They missed my school uniform vanishing and the thick woollen coat appearing in its place. And no one spotted my hair turn pale pink and wrap itself up in the purple headscarf.

In fact, I could have sat there for the whole lesson without anyone noticing, if I hadn't shouted: "Back in my day, this was all fields as far as the eye could see!"

I suddenly became aware that everyone was staring at me. One or two jaws even dropped.

"Excuse me..." said Mr Wells. "Can I help?"

Before I could reply, Owen jumped to his feet. "This is my granny!" he blurted out. "Billy had to go to the dentist at short notice and I brought my granny in to help me in school!"

Mr Wells blinked. "Help you?"

"Yes," said Owen. "You're allowed to take a dictionary into English class, and you can use calculators in maths... So I brought my granny in to help me in case there were any difficult bits in today's history lesson."

His voice wobbled a bit near the end of his explanation, but I had to give him top marks for quick thinking.

Everyone turned back to Mr Wells, waiting

for his reaction. It wasn't at all what I expected.

"What a marvellous idea!" he said, hurrying over. "Thank you for coming in, Mrs..."

"...Wrinkles," I said, glancing at the back of my hand. I know! But it was the first thing that came into my head.

"Mrs Wrinkles?" repeated the teacher.

"Yes," I said, smiling. There was no going back now. "But you can call me Doris!"

"OK then, Doris," said Mr Wells as he led me to the front of the class. "You say you can remember this area before the school was built, when it was just fields?"

"I can indeed!" I said, beginning to enjoy myself.

"And, when was that, if you don't mind my asking?"

I looked up at the topic Mr Wells had written on the board. "Oh, during the war."

Our teacher almost clapped his hands together with joy. "So you had first-hand experience of life in wartime?"

"Er ... yes," I said.

At the back of the room, Owen slid down in his chair.

"Then perhaps you can tell our pupils exactly what daily life was like during those dark years..."

"Yes, of course."

I smiled sweetly to my classmates, but inside I was screaming to myself: What

are you doing, you fool! You don't know
anything about the war apart from what
you've seen in old documentaries! Stop
talking and get out of here now!

I cleared my throat. "The main difference
between life today and back in the Second
World War was that ... er ... everyone in
wartime lived in black-and-white. The world
didn't turn to colour until the 1960s."

There was a flurry of scribbling as everyone wrote this down in their books.

"What?" said Mr Wells. I took his frown as a sign that I should continue.

"It wasn't easy, being in black-and-white," I explained. "Everyone was always getting cheese mixed up with soap, and it was impossible to play snooker 'cos all the balls looked the same, and rainbows were rubbish."

"No," said Mr Wells, gesturing for the class to put their pens down. "I don't think..."

But I was on a roll. "Everyone used to hope that they didn't get a Valentine's Day card on 14th February because they all had poems inside that started with 'Roses are grey, violets are grey...'"

"Thank you, Mrs Wrinkles!" said Mr Wells, ushering me towards the door.

I continued talking all the way. "It was really easy to get tomatoes confused with ping-pong balls, and all squirrels were grey, even the red ones."

Mr Wells pushed me out of the classroom and slammed the door. Seconds later, Owen was also thrown out, straining with my heavy handbag.

"So, what do we do now?" he asked, gladly handing the bag over.

I fixed him with a firm stare. "We go back to the source of the problem!"

We caught the bus to my granny's house. I found a senior citizen's bus pass at the bottom of my bag, along with enough loose change to pay for Owen. Luckily, we were alone on the top deck when I changed back again, and quickly lost fifty years.

We had just reached her door, when Gran opened it and smiled. "Billy," she said. "I've been expecting you. Hello, Owen. Come in, both of you."

I was halfway down the hall before I realised what she had said. "You called me Billy!" I gasped.

"Of course I did," said Gran. "You don't want me to use your full name and start another transformation to old age, do you?"

"So, that's what your trigger is!" cried
Owen. "It's when people call you Willia—"
Gran clamped a hand over his mouth before
he could finish saying my name.

"I said, we don't want Billy to change again! At least, not right now..."

We went into the kitchen, where my granny put the kettle on. "So, you know what's been happening to me?" I asked.

Gran nodded. "Exactly what I've been going through for the past 62 years," she said.

# Chapter Four: Battle!

I stared at her. "You're a were-granny, too?"

"Yes," she said, with a sigh. "I was bitten when I was just ten years old."

Owen scowled. "But, you're already... I mean, you aren't... What I mean is..."

"You mean I'm already old," said Gran, pouring the tea. "It is true that — if anyone ever calls me Elizabeth instead of Liz — I don't change much these days. But it was very different when I was younger. More difficult to conceal our precious gift."

"Gift!" I exclaimed, spitting out a mouthful of tea. "How can this be a gift?"

"You have been given special powers, Billy!" Gran said. "And, with great power—"

"I know this one!" grinned Owen. "It's from Spider-Man! With great power comes great responsibility!"

"No, that's not it," said my gran. "I was going to say — with great power, comes great big pants."

I blinked. "Pants?"

"Yes," said Gran. "That's your first lesson. Always wear big, comfortable pants when you're in your older form. You'll thank me one day."

"Lessons?" I queried. "You mean you're going to train me to be a granny?"

"I've already started!" said Gran, jumping up and grabbing her coat. "And we haven't a moment to lose. Follow me..."

So, Owen and I trailed after Gran as she dragged us to a coffee morning, knitting shop, bakery, charity store and bingo game.

She taught me which kind of boiled sweets to keep in my bag, how to correctly tuck a handkerchief up the sleeve of my cardigan, and when the best time was to shout at a group of youngsters hanging around on the street corner.

By the time we reached the bench outside the Post Office, I was exhausted! Owen and I collapsed.

"You two boys wait here while I nip in and pick up my pension," said Gran. "I didn't get the chance this morning."

I stretched out as she disappeared inside,

49

only for someone to trip over my feet as he
made to follow my granny.

"Watch it!" snarled a tall, thin guy.

"Sorry!" I said, pulling my feet in quickly.

The thin guy's mate — a short, chubby
man — glared at me as he scurried into the
Post Office after his friend.

I stretched out on the bench again, trying

50

to think of a way to change my name from William to Billy in the school register. If I could do that—

Wait a minute! Two men — one tall and thin, and the other short and chubby?

I grabbed the front of Owen's jumper. "I think the Post Office is about to be robbed!" I hissed.

"What?"

"Go and call the police!" I ordered. "I have to go and help my granny!"

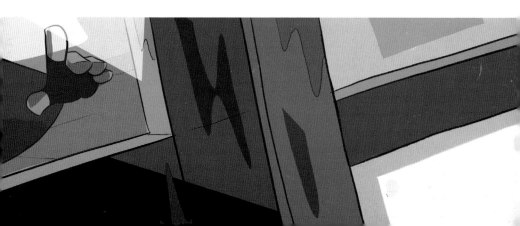

I crashed in through the doors of the Post Office just as the tall robber was tying up Mr Khan.

The other bad guy had hold of my granny's arm. "Lock the door behind you!" the villain snarled.

I did as I was told, locking the two robbers, Gran, Mr Khan and myself in the shop.

"Now, where's the safe?" said the thin guy, disappearing into the back room.

When he'd gone, Mr Khan turned to me and tried to talk through the gag over his face. "Mmmpph-mmph-mppphher-mphhheffmmpphhh."

Gran winked at me. "I think Mr Khan is

saying 'Good afternoon, Master William',"
she said.

"Quiet!" snapped the chubby robber.
"You three are our hostages. We'll do the...
talking..." His voice trailed away as my
transformation hit me with full force.

I bent over, ruffled my thin moustache, and then snapped my head up to glare at the bad guy through old lady eyes.

"Wh-what?" sputtered the chubby robber. "How did you...?"

"Let's just say we don't like it when things get granti-social!" I cackled.

"I presumed you'd just come in here for a STAMP!" snarled Gran, stomping on her captor's foot with a sensible shoe.

The fat guy yelled out in pain and began to hop around. I quickly pulled out a handful of boiled sweets from my handbag, and rolled them across the floor. I'm not sure exactly what kind of sweets grannies like to buy, but these things were indestructible. Instead of being crushed beneath the chubby robber's foot, he rolled on them and came crashing to the floor.

I took the opportunity to whack him a few times with my handbag, then I whipped off my headscarf and used it to tie his hands behind his back.

"Untie me, you old-aged weirdo!" the robber barked.

"You want to mind your language, sunshine!" I said. Then I whipped the snotty handkerchief from up my sleeve and stuffed it into his mouth.

Just then, the tall guy appeared from the back room. He had bundles of money piled high in his arms. He spotted his chubby friend on the floor and groaned. "Why have I always got to sort these things out myself?" he demanded, dumping the cash on the counter.

He stepped out from behind the till area — to find himself faced by my granny holding a pair of glinting knitting needles.

"What are you going to do with those things?" he chuckled. "Make me a sweater?"

"More like a straitjacket!" declared Gran, then she leapt into action. It was amazing! She was like some sort of knitting ninja

— dancing around her opponent in a blur, poking the needles through his jumper, grabbing lengths of wool and knitting them back in a new position.

Within minutes, the tall robber's arms were knitted behind his back, and his mouth was completely covered.

I slumped back against the wall as I changed back into a boy, just in time to see the police break down the Post Office door and rush inside. Owen was with them.

"You did it!" he cried as officers raced to untie Mr Khan. "You stopped them!"

I grinned. "Nothing your average were-granny couldn't handle!"

But Owen didn't reply. He was staring back out into the street at an old man wearing a green jacket.

"What's wrong?" I asked.

"You see that guy out there?" whispered Owen. "The one with the beard?"

I nodded. "What about him?"

Owen swallowed hard. "I think he might be a grampire!"

# TOMMY DONBAVAND'S FUNNY SHORTS

They'll have you in stitches!

978 1 4451 4676 8

978 1 4451 4673 7

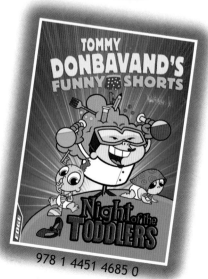

978 1 4451 4685 0